Uprooted

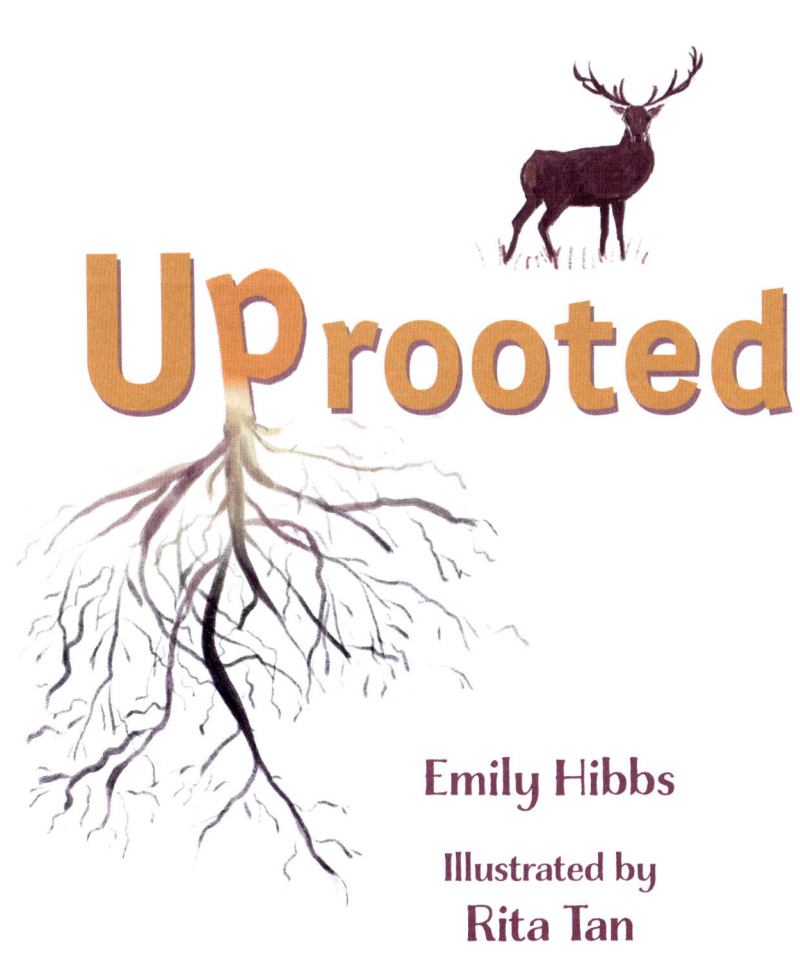

Emily Hibbs

Illustrated by Rita Tan

Collins

Contents

Ivy's nature Diary: Brookstone Woods 6

CHAPTER ONE Autumn 9

Ivy's nature Diary: 25th September 22

CHAPTER TWO Autumn 25

Ivy's nature Diary: 16th November 38

CHAPTER THREE Winter 41

Ivy's nature Diary: 15th January 54

CHAPTER FOUR Spring 59

Ivy's nature Diary: 2nd April 72

CHAPTER FIVE Summer 75

Ivy's nature Diary: 14th July 88

CHAPTER SIX Summer 91

About the author 106

About the illustrator 108

Book chat 110

Brookstone Woods

Nettle Pond

Kingfisher Bridge

Badger's Sett

CHAPTER ONE
Autumn

We lived in a cottage near the edge of the woods: Robin, Mum, Granny and me.

If that makes you think of fairy tales, then you're imagining it all wrong.

In fairy tales, the woods are wild and full of adventures. They aren't trapped behind metal fences. They don't have shouty signs saying:

And in fairy tales, nobody goes away to university or moves into a care home.

Are you imagining things differently now?

The changes started in September. "Autumn is a time of change," Granny always said. But she meant the leaves fading from green to gold, or the hedgehogs finding somewhere quiet to spend the cold months as the long nights slip in. She didn't mean these sorts of changes.

They began with a fall.

Granny hadn't hit her head, which was good, but she had broken her hip, which wasn't.

It happened the day before my big brother Robin was setting off for university, so the house already felt unsettled. Robin's bags were packed in the hall, but Granny hadn't tripped over them. She had got confused about which way her bedroom was again, she said. Got herself all turned around. Forgot that there was a step down into the kitchen. Missed it and fell.

At the hospital, a doctor showed us a grainy X-ray of the broken bone and Mum sucked in her breath noisily.

There would be an operation, and something called physiotherapy, which meant moving parts of your body in particular ways, again and again, until they were better. When the doctor mentioned 'around-the-clock care', Mum stiffened beside me.

The operation was scheduled for the next day, so Mum ended up having to go back to the hospital so she could be there when Granny woke up from it.

That meant Robin had to catch the train to university on his own, even though we were all supposed to go up with him.

We could tell Mum felt terrible – she went round in circles trying to come up with another plan until Robin squeezed her hand and said, "I'll be fine. Wren will help me with my stuff."

I'd nodded and said I would, and we'd both smiled strange stuck-on smiles.

Robin and I dragged his bags to the train station and up the stairs on to the platform. Robin didn't normally like hugs, but he let me squeeze him for a few seconds before letting go.

"You'll be all right?" he asked.

I tried to nod. Robin gave me a sideways look.

The doors began their closing *beep, beep, beep* and Robin jumped into the carriage. Once his train had slid out of sight, I walked home alone.

Noisy thoughts chased their tails inside my head. I reached the metal fence that caged in the woods and ran my fingers along it. Low branches poked through and a stone skittered under, soon lost among the litter of leaves.

I wondered what it would be like to step inside – to leave the pavement and disappear into somewhere wilder. But the fence must be there for a reason. And I wasn't sure I would, even if I could.

I didn't notice the boy until he was right in front of me. A streak of mud ran down one arm of his jumper, and his hair stuck up at the back like a bird whose feathers had been ruffled.

I recognised him from my new secondary school. He was always calling out answers before the teachers had finished their questions. The answers were usually right, at least, which seemed to annoy the teachers more than if they were wrong.

He grinned – a quick, fleeting thing – and walked past me, hands stuffed in his pockets. Had he come from the woods? I frowned, but he was gone when I turned back to look.

It was dark when Mum got home from the hospital. She sank down on the sofa beside me. "Well, Robin said his journey was smooth, and there are some friendly people on his corridor," she said. "And Granny's doing okay –"

Something about the way she hesitated made me sit up. "The operation went fine, but –" Mum twisted the bracelet I had made her around her wrist. "She's not very well, Wren."

Granny called it her 'little gremlin', the thing in her brain that stole her memories or jumbled them up. Sometimes it made her laugh, like the time she put the milk in the washing machine. But sometimes it made her cry, like when she forgot Robin's name for a moment on his birthday.

"She's going to need more help than we can manage here," Mum went on. "The doctors think a care home would be best, at least for now. There's a lovely one just down the road – Birchview. The staff seemed kind on the phone and there's a beautiful garden."

I wanted to shout and shake Mum's shoulders and say that, no, Granny couldn't move out. Her place was here. With us. But instead, I just asked in a small voice, "Will she like it there?"

Mum closed her eyes for a split-second too long. "She'll be safe, Wren. That's the most important thing. And we'll visit her all the time."

The next few days were a flurry of forms and phone calls with muffled sighs. As soon as she was well enough, Granny was going to move straight into the care home.

With Robin and Granny both gone, I wondered if this was how the last bird in a nest felt, left behind after the other fledglings had disappeared.

The next weekend, Granny was finally allowed to leave hospital. We picked her up and drove to Birchview. She sat in the passenger seat, her hands folded together in her lap, as we turned into the drive.

"Look, a wren," she said suddenly, pointing at the care home's chimney. "So I'll have my little songbird here with me, after all."

I squinted up at the sloping roof but couldn't see anything.

Mum and I helped Granny to her new room, which was small but sunny, with doors that opened onto the garden. One of the carers brought her tea and biscuits.

"It's like staying at a fancy hotel," she said, her eyes sparkling. I smiled back, but I couldn't help noticing how frail she seemed in this place, as if the faintest puff of breeze might carry her fluttering away.

Back at home that afternoon, Mum asked me to pick out a few books for Granny to have at Birchview. I flicked through her bookshelf, trying to decide which she might like. Beneath a pile of mystery stories, I found a weathered green notebook.

The paper inside was faded to yellow, as if it had soaked up years of sunlight. Granny's handwriting squiggled across the pages, along with delicate sketches of wildflowers and birds. Crumbling leaves, curled seed pods and a tiny snail shell were stuck down carefully.

At the front, there was a map with paths winding through trees.

It was our woods. The ones locked behind fences and warning signs.

Granny had explored them once.

And now, maybe I could, too.

25th September

The boy was in the woods again today. He still won't tell me his name, but he showed me the new entrance to the sett that the badgers dug. He said badger setts can be over a century old, handed down from generation to generation. I'm going to call him Badger Boy, because of the way he lights up when he talks about them, and the pale stripe running through his hair.

Together, we finished building my hedgehog home. We filled it with dry leaves and moss and tucked it into the roots of the hollow oak. It should be sheltered from the wind there. Badger Boy carved a tiny hedgehog on the side of the box, so they'll know it's for them. I hope they find it before the frost arrives.

A noisy jay collected acorns while we worked and left this behind.

CHAPTER TWO
Autumn

The diary stayed under my pillow at night, came with me to the kitchen table at mealtimes, and slipped into the zip pocket of my school bag. I read and reread it, until I could almost hear Granny's voice describing the early morning birdsong, the rain-soaked soil and the foxes with their fire-bright coats.

I didn't mention it to Mum, or to Robin, or even to Granny. It felt like something fragile, that might crumble if the wrong person looked at it.

Reading it filled the emptiness of our cottage. It made school seem less loud and packed full of people I didn't know how to talk to. At lunchtime, I'd flick through its pages and imagine the woods of sixty years ago.

I saw the boy with the muddy arm and sticky-up hair again. Then again. His name was Kai, and he was in two of my classes.

One Thursday morning in the middle of October, our science teacher, Mr Hall, announced we'd be studying habitats. Mr Hall was like a nature presenter on TV, all wide owl eyes and big, animated mouth. But when he said we'd need to get into pairs for a project, I felt a shiver of panic.

I sat on my own every lesson. Nobody was going to pick me.

"If I pair up with you, will you do all the writing?"

I looked up like a startled squirrel. The stool beside mine screeched against the floor as Kai dropped onto it, making everyone glance over.

I stared at him for a moment, "OK," I managed.

"I've seen your diary with drawings of animals in it and stuff." He pointed at the green notebook, which had escaped its zip pocket and was poking out of my bag. "Thought you'd be into this kind of thing."

"It's my granny's," I said quickly, pointing at the words 'Ivy's Diary' on the cover. "I'm just looking after it."

I wanted to ask him about the woods – about whether he'd been inside them.

"So, what local habitat do you want to write about?" Kai asked, before I could get the words out. "The pigeon nests in the bike sheds? Or I've heard a massive spider has made a lair in the girls' toilets."

A small laugh escaped before I could stop it. But Kai had already turned around to yell something across the classroom to his friend, the project forgotten.

That afternoon, I walked the long way home along the edge of the woods, even though the drizzle had turned to sleet and was falling in freezing flecks. The trees seemed to tug at me, the way they always did.

The fence was taller than I remembered, as if it had grown. I pressed my fingers against the cold metal, imagining a time when it wasn't here – when the trees stood unguarded and Granny could step straight into their shade without a second thought.

I didn't realise I was looking for something, until I found it. Near the place where I'd spotted Kai a few weeks ago. A gap in the fence, leaving an opening just big enough to crawl through.

I crouched down, the wet ground soaking through my tights and my heart *thud-thud-thudding*. Maybe I shouldn't. Maybe it wasn't safe. But the trees leaned a little closer, like they had secrets to share.

Before I could talk myself out of it, I ducked down and slipped through.

On this side of the fence, the world shifted. Clusters of red-and-white toadstools huddled at the base of a tree, like a fairy village. Silver puddles pooled between roots. My shoes sank into the spongy ground, mud oozing up around the laces.

"Well, hi there!"

I yelped and stumbled, arms windmilling. Kai leant against a tree, watching me. He had changed out of his school uniform and the hood of his jacket was pulled up.

"What are you doing here?" I blurted. For a moment, the woods had felt like just mine.

"I'm *always* here," he said. "What are *you* doing here? Thought you might be following me."

"I wasn't following you," I said quickly. "I was sort of following my granny."

The words spilled out before I could stop them. I told Kai about finding the diary. Then I told him about Granny's fall and her 'little gremlin' and about Robin and how our house felt like an empty nest since they had gone. It was like a dam had been broken inside me, and everything spilled out at once.

Kai tilted his head, studying me. "Fair enough. Welcome to the woods, then."

"It's amazing in here," I said before I could stop myself, then winced, worried Kai would laugh.

Instead, he crouched down and pointed to a shallow pit at the base of the tree, near the toadstool village. "See that? Badger scat."

I frowned and crouched beside him. "Badger what?"

"Poo," he said cheerfully. "You were about to kneel in it."

I jerked back so fast I almost went sprawling again. Kai laughed, the sound sharp and loud, like a crow call.

"Must be a sett nearby," he added.

I crouched down next to him again, carefully this time, squinting at a hole in the ground that could have been a sett entrance.

"They can be hundreds of years old," I said, remembering the note in Granny's diary.

I tried to imagine Granny standing in this exact spot, all those years ago, with Badger Boy pointing out the same signs. The past and present brushed against each other.

Kai let out a low, impressed whistle.
"We could write about badgers for our project? Or foxes! Or deer! There are loads of different animals that come through here."

"You know a lot about the woods," I said, watching him out the corner of my eye.

"I come here a lot," said Kai with a shrug. "It's quiet. In a good way. My house is the opposite – noisy, messy. You know…"

I nodded like I did and wondered if that was really why Kai had decided to pair with me. Perhaps, though he was loud, he was drawn to quiet things: places, people.

Then his face shifted, and he glanced over his shoulder, into the deeper woods. "There's someone else here, though. An old guy."

I glanced back through the trees. "Who is he?"

Kai shrugged. "Don't know. A wild man, maybe. Looks like he lives out here. I've kept out of his way. Not sure I want to find out."

The sleet had turned to rain. It trailed cold droplets down the back of my coat. The shadows stretched long and thin and black.

"I should get home," I said, the words coming out a bit shaky. "But maybe we could come here again. Together, I mean, to work on the project."

Kai grinned. "Deal. I'll do all the fun stuff – searching for tracks and building dens. You can write it up."

I rolled my eyes. But he had given me an idea. Perhaps I could retrace Granny's footsteps and try to finish some of the projects she started.

As I squeezed back through the hole in the fence, the branches above swayed like they were waving goodbye.

But it didn't feel like an ending. It felt like a beginning.

16th November

The woods are teetering between autumn and winter. The first frosts have set spiderwebs sparkling. We built a box for the robins and wrens and other birds that won't fly away to warmer places in the winter.

Badger Boy said he saw over fifty wrens huddled together in a hazel hollow last year.

While we worked, a flock of redwings darted between berries on the hawthorn bushes. They've come all the way from Scandinavia. We must remember to bring some seeds or apples when the weather gets colder and the berries have gone.

redwing

hawthorn

Even though everything looks dead, there is still so much life. Badger Boy says that, beneath the soil, the trees talk to each other. They are connected by fungi and share secret messages. I'm not sure if I believe him, but sometimes it does feel like the wood is whispering, so perhaps he is right.

Fly agaric; poisonous, don't touch!

CHAPTER THREE
Winter

Granny was always the brave one. The one to plunge into a river on a sunny day, while Robin dangled his toes on the bank, and I stood back, watching. She'd let spiders scuttle over her palms and strike up conversations with strangers.

I used to think that if I stayed close to her, some of that courage might rub off on me.

But at Birchview, everything was different. She seemed small for her chair and slow as she shuffled along the garden path with her new cane.

At our house, it was even worse. She'd sit politely at the kitchen table, sipping tea and staring around as though she'd never seen the place before.

The medicine for her hip blurred her thoughts. Her 'little gremlin' chased away the stories from her lips. Somehow, the girl in the diary – the one running through the woods with her pockets stuffed with treasures – felt more real than the Granny sitting in front of me. I wanted to find a way to bring her back.

One November afternoon, I visited her at Birchview without Mum. I pulled the diary out of my bag and passed it over. "Do you remember this?" I asked, waiting.

Her eyes widened. "Where did you find this?" she asked, flicking through. "Some of these drawings are dreadful!" She laughed and turned a sketch of a bat upside down.

"They're brilliant!" I protested.

She smiled, tracing the brittle petals and leaves. "Funny how these little pieces of the woods are still stuck here, frozen in time."

"I found a way into the woods," I told her. "Me and a boy from school. We're working on a school project, but we're exploring and helping wildlife too. Just like you and Badger Boy did. We found your bird box, and your hedgehog house and fixed them! And we built a new log pile for bugs."

Granny closed the diary with a thud that seemed too loud for such a small book. She handed it back to me.

"I'm glad you found my diary, but I wouldn't go into those woods anymore, songbird. They've been closed off for a reason."

I wanted to ask what she meant. To tell her how stepping into the woods felt like slipping inside her memories. But something in her voice held me back; it carried an ache.

Winter rushed in, all fierce frosts and bitter winds. Despite Granny's warnings, Kai and I kept going back to the woods. We'd meet just beyond the fence. For a while, we'd work on our badger project, but then we'd stay longer, retracing Granny and Badger Boy's footsteps. The diary became our guide, a kind of map.

To start with, we didn't talk much. In class, Kai filled every silence. In the woods, he didn't seem to feel the need to. But as time went on, we started sharing stories – about my hushed house, about Kai's chaotic one.

In Mr Hall's science lessons, we'd flick through Granny's diary under the desk, planning our next adventures.

Discovered a dormouse hibernating inside a pile of leaves. The little thing didn't even stir, but we could see its heart thumping inside its tiny body.

Just before Christmas, we handed in our project. Kai did most of the presenting while I stared at my shoes. Mr Hall beamed at us as we stood at the front of the class, but afterwards, he stopped us at the door.

"So, where exactly is this badger sett?" he asked, owl eyes blinking eagerly.

"Just … sort of near the edge of Brookstone Woods," Kai mumbled, his eyes darting to mine. We grabbed our bags and bolted before he could ask more.

"He'll think we've made it all up," I grumbled.

"Better that than getting in trouble for trespassing," Kai pointed out. "Do you want them to fix the fence so we can't get in?"

That afternoon, we hadn't planned to meet, but we ended up at the school gate at the same time. Kai fell into step beside me.

"Xbox at mine?" called one of Kai's friends, catching up.

"Another time," said Kai, slapping him on the back but keeping pace with me. I felt something loosen in my chest. "So, what shall we do today?"

We bounced ideas for projects back and forth, until we approached the woods.

"What I don't understand," I said, voicing something that had been puzzling me for a while, "is why the diary ends so suddenly."

"Maybe your granny ran out of paper."

I shook my head, and pulled out the diary to show him, flicking through the empty pages at the end.

"I'd like to meet her," Kai said. He checked nobody was looking, then squeezed through the gap.

"She's different now," I said, following him, the twisted metal catching on my bag.

I was in no rush to get home. Robin had been back for a week, but he was mostly studying in his room or out catching up with friends. Granny had been spending more time at our cottage, too. We'd brought in the Christmas tree from the garden and made gingerbread biscuits. It should have felt good, like we were getting back to normal. But it didn't feel right because this wasn't what normal was anymore.

Inside the woods, it was so cold that the air sparkled with tiny shards of glittering ice.

A dusting of frost clung to every tree's bark and branches, and even the stream had frozen over. The cold seeped in the gaps between my gloves and coat. We filled a bird feeder and checked that the entrance to the hedgehog house was still clear.

"I'm not really looking forward to the holidays," Kai said quietly, echoing my own thoughts, as we walked back towards the hole in the fence.

"We can still come to the woods," I reassured him. "Wish you had a phone, though. Then we could plan it."

"We'll be like your granny and Badger Boy – if I see you, I see you," Kai said. "Maybe we could leave each other notes, like they did!"

Granny's diary told of a secret hiding place where she and Badger Boy had left treasures for each other, but we hadn't found it yet.

"Look," Kai said, his voice taut. I followed his gaze to the ground. It was twilight but I could still make out the footsteps in the frost.

"The wild man," I said, nudging them with my toe.

We sped up, but a few seconds later Kai held up a hand to stop me. My heart pounded, but then I heard it, too. Like a faint applause but coming from above. I looked up.

For a moment, I thought that black leaves were falling from the trees – only, they were falling upwards. Then I saw, they weren't leaves, but birds. Hundreds of them, creating an inky smudge against the sky.

We followed them through the trees, watching snatches of them through the branches, shifting from a tight, pulsing ball to a snaking ribbon. For a moment, I forgot the cold, forgot everything.

When they finally disappeared over the treetops, I felt lighter somehow.

15th January

We followed heart-shaped deer tracks in the snow to Kingfisher Bridge, the water in the stream frozen in glassy waves. Badger Boy dared me to test the ice with a stick. He always dares me, but I don't always say yes.

roe deer tracks

Nearby, we saw some tiny claw prints. Badger Boy thinks they might belong to a pine marten, but we couldn't be sure.

pine marten tracks?

more on the next page

Later, as the sky turned pink and purple, a murmuration of starlings swept across it. I read once that they might fly like that to confuse predators. But maybe they just like to dance.

ivy leaf

I've been coming to the woods on my own more, as Badger Boy says he can't come as much, though he won't say why. I leave him treasures in our secret letter box, the hollow in the hazel tree. Today, after he left, I found the biggest pinecone I'd ever seen and put it there.

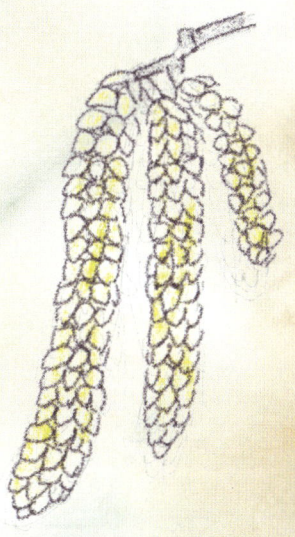

hazel catkins ('lamb's tails') are starting to appear

CHAPTER FOUR
Spring

January slipped into February, then February into March. The days began to stretch.

We decided to find Granny and Badger Boy's hiding place. She'd written about it so often that it felt like something from a legend.

To start with, we worked out which trees were hazel trees. They still had no leaves, but fluffy golden tails trailed from their branches. Suddenly, the woods seemed full of them, and we searched each one for a hidden hollow. Some afternoons, it felt like a treasure hunt. Other afternoons, it felt totally pointless. Sixty years was a long time. Maybe a storm had torn the tree from the ground and now it was just one of the rotting logs that littered the floor.

Badger Boy left me a
jackdaw's feather in
our hiding place today.
It shimmered green and
purple in the sunlight.

I left him half a blackbird
eggshell in return,
sky-blue and speckled.

Then, one day, we found it.

Somehow I knew, even before we properly looked. It was on the edge of a clearing, in the place marked as *Wren's Perch* on Granny's map.

The trunk was half-hidden behind a tangle of ivy. Bark had grown over most of the hollow, leaving a narrow gap. I stretched up and squeezed my hand inside.

Something soft brushed my fingers, then something small and skittering – a spider, maybe. I yelped and jerked back, shaking my hand furiously as Kai doubled over with laughter.

"Your turn," I said, trying to glare at him while the corners of my mouth curled upwards.

We swapped places, and Kai reached into the hollow, his hand disappearing into the tree. "There's definitely something here," he said, his voice suddenly serious. "But I can't … quite…" He grimaced, stretching his arm further.

"Let me try again," I said.

Kai stepped aside, and I wriggled my fingers deep into the space. At first, I felt only rough wood and damp moss, but then, at the very back, my hand closed around something square-edged. I drew it out.

It was a small leather envelope, cracked at the edges. A strap bound it closed. My fingers trembled as I untied it.

"This is epic," Kai breathed, peering over my shoulder.

Inside was a folded letter. The paper was stained brown by water that must have seeped in, but I could still make out the handwriting. It was messier than Granny's, as if whoever had written it had been in a rush. I began to read:

20th July

Dear Ivy,

I want to start by saying, I'm sorry. I'm sorry for what I said, and for what happened. I know you think I didn't do enough to stop it, but I'm not brave like you. I might swing over streams or climb tall trees, but I don't have your kind of courage.

I was scared. Scared of what my family would say, what they'd do, if I went against their wishes. But I regret it.

I wish things had stayed the same, that nothing had changed. The thought of never seeing you again, of never exploring the woods together, makes me feel lost.

I hope you'll find your way back. I hope you'll find this letter.

Yours,

Badger Boy

I read the letter quickly, then slowly out loud. It scratched at my brain.

"Do you think that this is why your granny stopped writing in the diary?" asked Kai. "It sounds like something happened, and she stopped coming to the woods."

My thoughts tangled and twisted, like roots reaching for water in the dark.

"What are you going to do?" Kai asked.

I didn't answer. Part of me wanted to run straight to Birchview and show Granny. But another part hesitated. Would it hurt her to read it? Would it confuse her? Maybe the woods had kept it hidden for a reason.

"I'll ask my mum," I said quietly. She still didn't know about our visits to the woods, but this felt too big to handle on our own.

We took the letter back to the cottage. Mum was already home, chopping peppers while pasta bubbled on the hob. I paused in the doorway, still clutching the letter.

She glanced up and smiled, her eyes flicking to Kai. If she was relieved I'd finally brought a friend home, she didn't let on. "You two have been out late. What've you been up to?"

Before I could answer, Robin's voice called out hello from her phone. He waved from the screen, and I tried to wave back, but my hand shook so much it was more of a flap.

Mum turned back to the phone, stirring the pasta. "And then there's the housing development planned for the old woods," she said to Robin, tossing the peppers into the pan. They hit the oil with a sharp sizzle. "It's going to be chaos once the builders get started."

"What?" I blurted, louder than I meant to.

Mum glanced up. "The land's being sold to developers. I heard at work today."

Her words felt like being plunged into a freezing stream. "They can't just ... destroy it!"

Kai didn't say anything, but his fingers curled tightly around the edge of the kitchen table.

"It's already fenced off, love. Nobody uses it." She turned back to the stove. "There's plenty of pasta here if your friend is hungry. And what are you having for dinner, Robin? I hope you're eating properly."

I didn't answer. Kai still hadn't spoken, and for some reason, that annoyed me. I grabbed his wrist and dragged him outside to the garden. My breath came fast and sharp, puffing little clouds of panic into the air.

"We've got to do something," I said. "They can't sell our woods."

Kai rocked on his heels.

"Wren, they're not really *our* woods. There's nothing we can do. We're just kids."

Everything was bright and loud and my head was full of thunder. The world was tilting, slipping – about to fall apart – and somehow Kai was just stood there.

"But what about the badgers? And the starlings and the deer and the hedgehogs? And what about the trees! They've been there for so long, Kai!"

Kai let out a slow breath. "Hey, it's not the end of the world, Wren."

"It is to me!" I shouted. "But if you'd rather give up, then go ahead – just leave! Go back to your noisy house and your stupid Xbox."

Kai's eyes flashed, but he didn't say anything. He turned and walked away, leaving me standing there on our garden path with the letter crumpled and hot in my hand.

When Mum called me in for dinner, she frowned at the empty chair beside mine. "Where's your friend?"

"He had to go home," I muttered. "But he's not really my friend. Just a boy from school I did a project with."

She didn't push me, and I didn't offer anything more. But the way I'd snapped at Kai stuck with me, like a snagged bramble.

Upstairs, I slid the letter into the diary and tucked them both under my pillow.

The woods were changing.

And so was everything else.

2nd April

The woods are awake now. Little splashes of colour have appeared everywhere. Purple primroses dust the ground, fresh pink hawthorn blossoms brighten the bushes, and yellow crocuses peek through the frost.

primroses

Then there are the greens — emerald and jade and sage and lime and a thousand other shades I don't have a name for — bursting from bushes, unfurling along branches and wriggling their way through the soil.

cuckoo

We heard the cuckoo calling again — its two-note song floated over the treetops, clear and confident.

The first froglets have emerged from the pond we dug, their tiny legs working hard.

Badger Boy didn't talk as much as usual. He stayed beside Nettle Pond after I left, staring into the water as if it might show him something. I hope he's not tired of the woods. Or tired of me.

CHAPTER FIVE
Summer

"Swifts!" I cried, pointing at the birds swooping through the sky on black crescent wings above Birchview.

Granny followed my finger. "Swallows," she corrected gently. "Longer tails and white tummies."

"Swallows," I amended, and we watched them wheel and swoop, snapping insects from the air.

I wondered if they were heading for the woods, and what would happen to them once the diggers and destruction started. Would they still come next year if the trees were gone?

I hadn't talked to anyone about the sale of the woods. I didn't think Mum or Robin would understand, and I didn't know what feelings it would stir up in Granny.

I added it to the list of things I was keeping from her, along with Badger Boy's letter.

"You're quiet today, songbird," Granny said, her eyes still fixed on the birds above.

Some days, she told the same story three times, or forgot why she'd walked into a room. But today, she was just … Granny. We sat sipping water with ice and lemon, leaning back on two deckchairs in Birchview's garden, as if we were on holiday.

"I'm just thinking," I said. "About things changing."

Granny hummed, she turned and met my eyes. "You know, the winds shift, the seasons turn, and the swallows move on. Change isn't always something to fight, songbird – it's sometimes something to fly with."

The date of the sale crept up: a big X in my calendar.

It hadn't rained in weeks. The grass in the garden had turned crispy and brown, and the leaves in the woods hung limp and thirsty.

It was as if everything was holding its breath.

I had trawled through the development plans online. Complicated drawings of houses squeezed in tight. Long, winding sentences stuffed with confusing phrases. I had written letters – to the council, our MP, the housing company.

I told them about the badgers, the deer, the starlings in their sweeping murmurations. I didn't lie, but I chose my words carefully, to make it sound like I'd spotted all these things through the fence. Their replies all sounded the same.

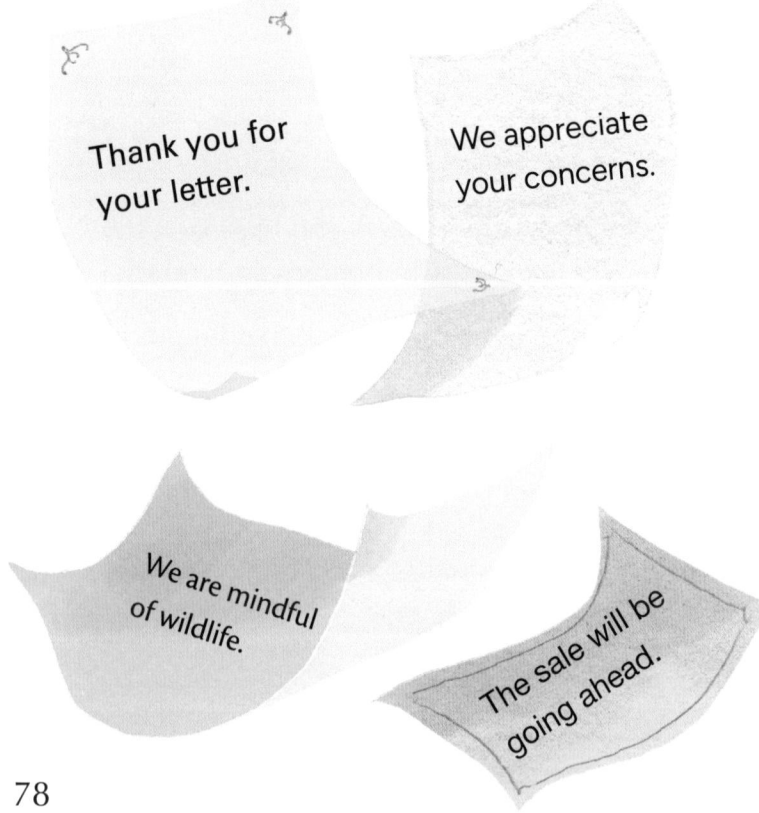

Thank you for your letter.

We appreciate your concerns.

We are mindful of wildlife.

The sale will be going ahead.

I wanted to write to the landowner, but I couldn't find out who they were. Kai and I had glimpsed a big house through the trees once, but the fence separated us from it.

I'd always been someone who noticed things but didn't speak up. This time, I had tried to do something. And it had changed nothing.

The last day before the sale, it was the summer solstice. The longest day the woods would have this year, and the last. After school, I slipped through the fence for a final time.

The woods felt strange. Heavy clouds hung low. The wind was picking up, making the leaves whisper like worried murmurs. I could feel a storm was coming – the air was charged. But I had to say goodbye.

My eyes stung, and I knew it wasn't just the floating tree pollen.

"Hi there," a voice behind me said. My heart lifted a little.

"What are you doing here?" I asked without turning around.

"Same thing you are," replied Kai. "Saying goodbye."

I nodded, but didn't trust that I would get any words out over the lump in my throat.

"I wrote to the council, you know," said Kai, and I turned to face him. He had his hands stuffed deep in his pockets and was kicking at the ground, sending out puffs of dust which caught the light. "I got Mr Hall to check it sounded OK."

"I wrote to them, too," I said.

"Didn't exactly work, did it?" Kai tried to smile.

"It's not fair," I said, finally voicing all the thoughts that I had been trying to squish down inside me. "These woods don't *belong* to anyone. A piece of paper can't change that, and neither can a fence. Woods are their own places. They belong to everyone, and to no one."

"I know."

I felt hot, angry tears sliding down my face.

"And I'm not just crying about the woods," I said, brushing at my cheeks impatiently.

"I know, Wren."

We began walking in silence, our feet following our favourite paths without us having to exchange a word. At the badger sett, we hesitated. The woods were too still. A place that had always been full of life now felt … afraid. Perhaps the trees were sending secret messages to each other beneath the soil, like they knew what was coming.

"I'm sorry," I said.

Kai looked up. "What for?"

"For shouting at you. For expecting you to feel exactly the same as me." I let out a tight breath. "I don't even know how I feel half the time."

Kai kicked at the dry earth again. "I get it."

A sharp crack shattered the quiet as a branch snapped underfoot.

We spun around.

A man burst through the trees.

He was wearing a long, ragged coat, despite the heat, and his speckled grey hair seemed to grow outwards, rather than downwards. His mouth was twisted in a shout, the words lost in the wind that had surged, making the branches above creak and sway.

He called out again and lurched towards us. Kai looked at me, his eyes startled.

"Run!" he shouted, grabbing my arm and tugging. We tore away through the trees, dipping and diving through the trunks, taking different routes then drawing back together. I hadn't realised how well I knew these half-paths and maze-like deer tracks until I was running them at full pelt. But brambles snatched at my sleeves and roots seemed to rise up, as if the woods were trying to hold us back.

"Wren!" Kai called out from somewhere just behind me. I turned to see him sprawled on the ground, clutching his ankle.

I hesitated for half a second, then ran back, hauling him up. Kai managed to stand but let out a low moan as he tried shifting his weight onto the ankle he had fallen on.

"Stop!" another voice called breathlessly. The wild man was approaching, with uneven, staggering steps. "Wait! I'm not trying to frighten you!"

Kai and I exchanged a glance. Up close, he looked a little less wild. His dark, pebble-grey hair had a streak of white running through it, just like a—

"I'm trying to warn you! You need to get out the woods," the man said. "The storm. It's not safe to be under the trees if lightning strikes."

As if his words had given it permission, the sky crackled with a low rumble of thunder.

Kai winced, shifting his foot beneath him.

The man nodded. "Let's get your friend somewhere safe. Then we can come up with a plan."

A fat raindrop fell on my cheek. The thought that had been tugging at the edges of my brain suddenly sharpened. I looked at the pale streak in his hair again.

My fingers tightened around the diary in my pocket.

"Badger Boy?"

The man turned to look at me, really look at me.

Finally, he replied. "I haven't been called that in a very long time."

14th July

The woods are transformed once again. Bees and butterflies hum and flutter between the wildflowers. Dragonflies and damselflies flit over the pond we built, all shimmering wings and long limbs.

This dragonfly's last flight had ended before I found it — I pressed it here so it won't be forgotten.

When I stay late into the evenings, tiny bats, no bigger than my thumb, flit between the treetops, feasting on all the insect life. They have bat pups to raise and are very busy. The rains are few and far between, but the thirsty woodland laps them up.

pipistrelle bat

Spotted a skin that a slow worm had shed on the path, ghostly and delicate. I scooped it up, but it was too fragile to stick in.

I've hardly seen Badger Boy these last few weeks. He's turns up late, or leaves early, or doesn't make an appearance at all. But he left a note in our hiding place, telling me to meet him here, tonight. Something about the shortness of the note, or the haste of his handwriting, has me worried that something is about to change. I hope I'm wrong.

CHAPTER SIX
Summer

It ended with a fall.

Kai had twisted his ankle badly and could barely limp. Badger Boy and I took an arm each, supporting him as we made our way through the woods.

Instead of heading for the usual gap, we followed a different path. Here, the trees were thicker, the fence higher.

Rain hammered down as Badger Boy fished out a key from his coat pocket. He unlocked a gate, pushing it open with a low creak. Beyond lay a sprawling lawn and, beyond that, the grand house Kai and I had glimpsed through the trees.

I stared.

"You live here?" Kai asked, eyebrows shooting up.

Badger Boy didn't answer. He helped Kai across the grass, up the stone steps, and into the house. I knew we shouldn't go into a stranger's home, but Kai's ankle was swelling and the rain was pouring down.

Inside, the air smelled damp. Sheets covered the furniture and a stag's head loomed from the wall.

Badger Boy left, then returned moments later, crouching beside Kai to wind a bandage around his ankle. I reached for my phone to message Mum or offer it to Kai to call home, but my battery was dead.

"Cool house," Kai muttered through gritted teeth as Badger Boy tugged the bandage tight.

Badger Boy snorted. "Never liked it here. The woods always felt more like home."

I turned to him, piecing the puzzle together. "Do you own the woods, then? Was it you who fenced them off?"

Badger Boy let out a slow breath. "Not me. My father. Lord Brookstone." His gaze flicked to the stag's head. "He wasn't a nature lover. He liked owning things – wanted to keep the estate his and his alone. The fence was his way of keeping people out. If he could have kept the wildlife out, I bet he would have done that, too."

The fence made the woods feel like a secret place – but also trapped. A cage around something untameable.

Badger Boy went on. "When the fence went up, I stopped going in. It didn't feel the same, without the walkers, without Ivy. Not long after, my father sent me to boarding school, and I've hardly been back since. I only returned when the developers started sniffing around. I wanted to sell – to be rid of the whole place. The house, the woods, the memories."

"But it shouldn't be yours to give away!" I burst out, surprising myself as my voice rose. "It belongs to all the creatures living in it. It's their home. If you sell it, it'll be torn apart."

"You should fight for the woods," Kai said quietly. "Like Wren's granny wanted you to."

Badger Boy looked at me, and I knew he was searching for Granny in my face.

He nodded. "I see it now. The same sharp eyes. Piercing, just like Ivy's."

His words warmed and unsettled me all at once.

"She still lives nearby," I said. "At Birchview Care Home. She never read your letter."

"We fell out," he admitted. "I told her what my father planned to do, and she was furious. She wanted me to stand up for the woods, but I didn't know how. When I let her down, I suppose she didn't try to find me again."

He exhaled and ran a hand through his streaked hair. "She didn't even know my real name. It's Arthur. Arthur Brookstone."

I held out the diary to him. It felt warm, like a living thing.

"What your family did all those years ago wasn't right. But what you're doing – selling the woods – is worse," I said.

Arthur took the diary and thumbed through the pages. He smiled at some of the things Granny had written, and at one point, even laughed aloud.

"You know," he said at last, closing the book gently, "I'd noticed someone fixing things in the woods. Thought I saw you a couple of times, but you were always too quick. Like forest fairies."

Arthur smiled, then suddenly stopped. "I wouldn't know where to start. I can't undo the past." He glanced out the window.

"I think the rain is easing," he said. "Can I give you both a lift home?"

Outside, the storm had softened into a thin silver mist. The trees above the fence looked greener, washed fresh by the rain.

I took a deep breath. It wasn't over yet. I had a single, short car journey to persuade him.

The next day, I walked with Granny from her room to where Arthur was waiting. He clutched a bunch of woodland flowers.

"We've brought someone to see you," I said softly. "His name's Arthur, by the way."

Kai gave Arthur a gentle nudge forward.

For a moment, Granny only studied him, her expression unreadable. Then, slowly, a grin spread across her face. It wasn't a small, polite smile, but a wide, wild one.

"Hello, old friend," she said.

"Hello, Ivy," said Arthur. Granny stepped forward and wrapped her arms around him. He was two heads taller, but somehow she didn't look small as she hugged him tight.

"Your granddaughter has given me a serious talking to," Arthur said. Granny shot me a look, but I could tell she wasn't cross.

"I've decided to listen this time. I'm sorry I didn't listen to you all those years ago. You might have heard I was selling the family's woodlands. Well, I'm not going to. I've spoken to the developers. I'm keeping the land and I'm granting it special protection. I'm going to look after the woods again – and invite others in to help."

Granny's sharp eyes sparkled. "Better late than never, Badger Boy." She patted his arm. "And I know a few people here who'd love to be involved."

A few weeks later, we stood at the edge of the woods: Arthur, Granny, Robin, Mum, Kai and me. Summer was starting its slow shift into autumn. Long shadows stretched in the golden light, and the leaves had begun their gentle fade.

Granny had her cane, but she stood tall as we stepped through the new gate in the fence. A sign beside it listed the evenings and weekends the woods would be open for wildlife tours and conservation events.

I watched as Granny walked beneath the trees she hadn't seen in sixty years.

"It's all still here," she said, her fingers trailing down a silver birch. "And yet, it's all different."

She reached for my hand. "Thank you, songbird."

She might not always remember this moment, but I would. And for now, that was enough.

I thought about what she had said before, about change. Some things you had to fight against. But some you had to fly with. I knew that one day, Granny might not know my name, or even who I was. And that would be sad. But it would be OK.

I'd sit with her and listen to the birds. I'd read to her from her diary and tell her what I'd seen and heard in the woods.

I closed my eyes and listened – to the hum of the trees, to the world still turning.

Somewhere overhead, a blackbird sang its last song of the day.

About the author

When did you know you wanted to be an author?

Emily Hibbs

I don't really remember a time when I didn't want to be an author! As soon as I learned to read and write, I started making up stories – scribbling in notebooks and even illustrating them (badly!). But it took me a long time to actually become an author. Before that, I worked as an editor, helping other writers make their books the best they could be. I think you have to be a little bit brave to share your own writing, and it took me a while to build up the courage.

Is anyone in this story based on a real person?

I had two wonderful grandmothers – Hazel and Joan – who inspired parts of Ivy. My grandma Hazel had dementia later in life, just like Ivy, and she moved into a care home. She also broke her hip (though in real life, it happened after she moved, not before). It was a hard time for my family, but we still found moments of joy.

We liked walking in the care home's garden, and even when my grandma's memory faded, she'd always ask if I had written any books lately. And if I had, she insisted she must have a copy!

What do you enjoy most about writing books?
I love creating new worlds and characters in my head, then turning that jumble of ideas into a story. I also love it when something clicks – a sentence that finally sounds right, a character who suddenly feels real, or a tiny detail that ties the whole story together.

How did you come up with the idea for this book?
During the Covid-19 pandemic, I lived in a small flat in Bristol. When we were allowed outside more, I found myself noticing nature in a way I hadn't before. I started keeping a nature diary, just like Wren's granny, writing down what I saw and paying attention to the wildlife I came across. I think being in nature helps us feel grounded, even when everything else is shifting. And that's where this story began.

Do you have a favourite part of the story?
I like writing beginnings and endings best. The beginning of a story is like stepping into a new world – getting to know the characters and setting the scene. The ending is always bittersweet, but it's satisfying giving my characters a proper goodbye. And I really love writing about nature, remembering special things I've spotted, or interesting facts I've learned, and finding ways to include them in my writing.

What do you hope readers will get out of the book?
I hope this book makes you curious about the wild spaces in your area, and the details in nature we often miss, like a snippet of birdsong or the first bud in spring. I also hope it brings comfort to anyone going through changes – big or small.

About the illustrator

Did you always want to be an illustrator?

I've always loved to draw since I was a child. I could spend hours drawing, but I never thought about becoming an illustrator. I wasn't brave enough. I chose a safer career in the software industry, my drawing book and pencils were forgotten for a long time.

Rita Tan

How did you get into illustrating?

You could say that the picture books my children had sparked my passion again. They spoke of my childhood memories — happy memories of drawing. I wanted to feel that joy again. So this time, I was going to be brave and I finally picked up my pencils again.

How do you go about illustrating a book like this?

I start with the characters and what they might look like. Once I have the characters, then I imagine the settings. A lot of the settings in this book were inspired by the forests near my home. Some of the trees have curious shapes which are so memorable, I tried to include them in this book. For example, a nearby park has a tree that resembles an elephant head, and my children's school has a giant tree that looks like a banana. Maybe you can spot them in this book!

Do you prefer to work digitally or with paper, pencils and paint?
It changes over time. When I was little I really, really loved pastels. Not long after that, I found marker pens and couldn't get enough of them. Then I started liking watercolour and its dreamy transparency. Lately I'm drawn to gouache and ink. Who knows what else I will favour next time. Even now, when I draw mostly digitally, I find I still yearn to draw with traditional media.

What was your favourite part of this book to illustrate?
Definitely the woods!

Does anything you've drawn relate to your own life or experiences?
I grew up in a city of concrete and malls. When I was little my idea of a forest was my grandmother's garden, tucked in between tall, neighbouring walls of bricks behind roaring traffic. My mother, my sister and I would fight through traffic jams to get to her house. As soon as we stepped into her front garden, the scorching heat of the day, the blaring car honks and the swerving motorcycles seemed to melt away. We were greeted by my grandmother's lush overgrown (but well tended) garden and clouds of mosquitos. My grandmother was an avid gardener (she didn't need the internet to find out how to care for a plant, she was a natural). I'd like to think she could just whisper to a plant and it would grow. She gardened until old age and dementia stopped her. I'd like to bring that memory of her garden's lushness into this book to remember her.

Book chat

What did you think this book might be about when you saw the cover and title? Were you right?

How did Wren change from the start of the book to the end?

Do you have a favourite season? Why do you like it?

If you could step inside this book for a day, which scene would you want to experience?

Who would you recommend this book to and why?

Wren sometimes compares herself to her granny. Do you have a family member you look up to? What do you admire about them?

If you could ask the author anything, what would you ask?

If you had to choose a different title for this book, what would you call it and why?

Book challenge:

Sit for a few minutes and sketch something from nature like Ivy's nature diary.

Published by Collins
An imprint of HarperCollins*Publishers*

The News Building
1 London Bridge Street
London
SE1 9GF
UK

Macken House
39/40 Mayor Street Upper
Dublin 1
D01 C9W8
Ireland

Text © Emily Hibbs 2025
Design and illustrations © HarperCollins*Publishers* Limited 2025

10 9 8 7 6 5 4 3 2 1

ISBN 978-0-00-876784-6

All rights reserved. No part of this publication may be reproduced, stored in a retrieval system, or transmitted in any form by any means, electronic, mechanical, photocopying, recording or otherwise, without the prior written permission of the Publisher or a licence permitting restricted copying in the United Kingdom issued by the Copyright Licensing Agency Ltd, 5th Floor, Shackleton House, 4 Battle Bridge Lane, London SE1 2HX.

Without limiting the author's and publisher's exclusive rights, any unauthorised use of this publication to train generative artificial intelligence (AI) technologies is expressly prohibited. HarperCollins also exercise their rights under Article 4(3) of the Digital Single Market Directive 2019/790 and expressly reserve this publication from the text and data mining exception.

British Library Cataloguing-in-Publication Data
A catalogue record for this publication is available from the British Library.

Download the teaching notes and word cards to accompany this book at:
http://littlewandle.org.uk/signupfluency/

Get the latest Collins Big Cat news at
collins.co.uk/collinsbigcat

Author: Emily Hibbs
Illustrator: Rita Tan (Illo Agency)
Publisher: Laura White
Commissioning editor and
 product manager: Caroline Green
Series editor: Charlotte Raby
Development editor: Catherine Baker
Project manager: Emily Hooton
Copyeditor: Sally Byford
Proofreader: Catherine Dakin
Cover designer: Sarah Finan
Typesetter: 2Hoots Publishing Services Ltd
Production controller: Katharine Willard

Printed in the UK.

MIX
Paper | Supporting
responsible forestry
FSC™ C007454

This book contains FSC™ certified paper and other controlled sources to ensure responsible forest management.

For more information visit: www.harpercollins.co.uk/green

Made with responsibly sourced paper and vegetable ink

Scan to see how we are reducing our environmental impact.